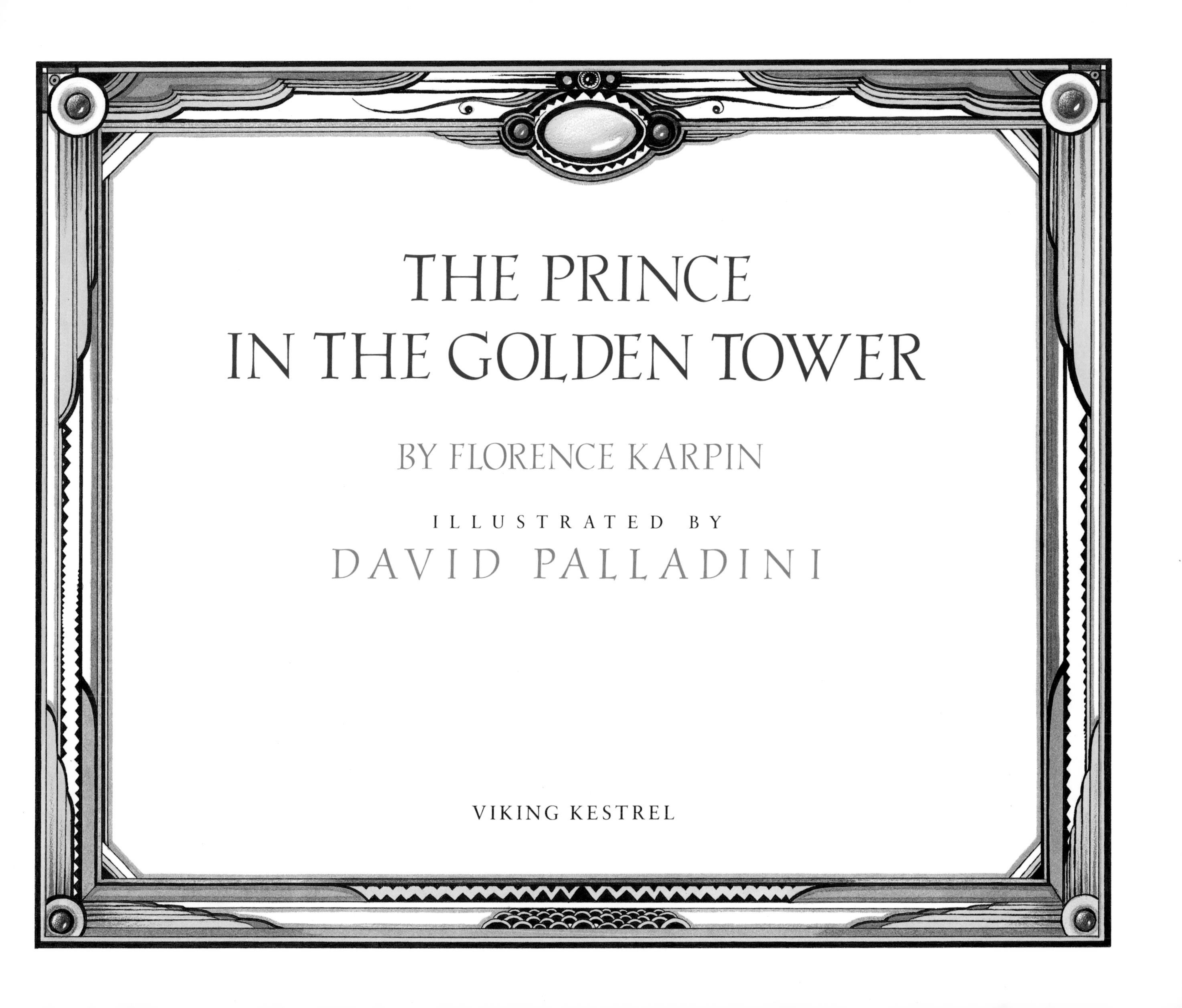

THE PRINCE IN THE GOLDEN TOWER

BY FLORENCE KARPIN

ILLUSTRATED BY
DAVID PALLADINI

VIKING KESTREL

For Jasmin and for Mischa F.K.

For Sherry, my true love D.P.

The art was rendered in markers, ink, and pencil on Strathmore Bristol paper.

VIKING KESTREL
Published by the Penguin Group
Viking Penguin, a division of Penguin Books USA Inc.,
40 West 23rd Street, New York, New York 10010, U.S.A.
Penguin Books Ltd, 27 Wrights Lane, London W8 5TZ, England
Penguin Books Australia Ltd, Ringwood, Victoria, Australia
Penguin Books Canada Ltd, 2801 John Street, Markham, Ontario, Canada L3R 1B4
Penguin Books (N.Z.) Ltd, 182–190 Wairau Road, Auckland 10, New Zealand

Penguin Books Ltd, Registered Offices: Harmondsworth, Middlesex, England

First published in 1989 by Viking Penguin, a division of Penguin Books USA Inc.
10 9 8 7 6 5 4 3 2 1

LIBRARY OF CONGRESS CATALOGING-IN-PUBLICATION DATA
Karpin, Florence B. The prince in the golden tower
by Florence B. Karpin : pictures by David Palladini. p. cm.
ISBN 0-670-82218-3 [1. Fairy tales.] I. Palladini, David, ill. II. Title.
Summary: Protected from all evil and knowledge of the world since his birth, Prince Sanjay finds both his life and the fate of the kingdom changed after a white tiger takes him on a fantastic journey.
PZ8.K2209Pr 1989 [E]—dc20 89-9033
Printed in Japan.
Set in Sabon.

nce, a long time ago, an Emperor who ruled a faraway land summoned seven thousand of his workers to build him a palace of gold. After many years of toil, the task was done, and the palace stood high above the jungle like a brilliant jewel upon the mountain.

Within its golden towers were rooms laden with treasure which the Emperor had plundered from lesser kingdoms, and deep in the cellars were huge vaults filled with chests of gold coins. The chambers were all of gold, and every winding stair and pillared arch was embellished with precious gems and pearls.

Amid this resplendence lived the Emperor, with his seven wives and forty-nine daughters. Yet the Emperor was not content. He wished only for a son, an heir to his golden empire, for in that eastern land, only men might rule.

Each day at dawn and dusk, he would go to the golden temple and beg the great Nurvah, god of Creation and Destruction, to send him a son. "O great and wondrous god, heed my prayer," wailed the Emperor, "and I will gladly give my gold to the poor unfortunates outside my palace walls."

At last a son was born, and the little prince was named Sanjay. The Emperor, his wish for an heir fulfilled, denied his promise to Nurvah, and kept his gold.

Prince Sanjay grew to be a beautiful child, with eyes like amber and hair as dark as midnight. His kind and cheerful nature was like a sunny morning, endearing him to all.

To all but the Emperor. Though proud and boastful of his son, he looked upon the boy only as security for his golden empire, and nothing more.

On the day the prince reached his seventh birthday, his father summoned him to his chambers. The Emperor, lounging upon silken pillows amid his seven doting wives, announced coldly, "Sanjay, my son, this day shall mark the first of your days in the high tower. There you will live, henceforth, until you ascend the golden throne." The seven wives gasped behind their veils, but dared not protest.

"But Father . . ." began the boy.

"I have spoken!" bellowed the Emperor.

And being a good and obedient son, the young prince dutifully climbed the seventy-seven steps that wound up and up, all the way to the top of the golden tower.

For a time, the prince was content in his airy room. His seven mothers and his forty-nine sisters tended to his every wish, and nothing was spared to please him. They made him clothes of the finest silks and brocades. They read him stories. They taught him music. For his amusement, brilliant birds of the jungle were housed in golden cages, while peacocks and playful monkeys roamed the golden hall.

Even so, as he grew from boyhood, Sanjay began to tire of his confinement. Each day, he became more restless, and spent long hours gazing from his high window.

One night, when the moon was full, the prince glimpsed something white moving far below in the shadow of the mountain. As he peered more closely, it suddenly vanished before his eyes. Each night thereafter the prince watched eagerly from his window. But the vision did not come again, and soon the moon waned.

Then came a night when the mountain was again bathed in silvery light. Prince Sanjay was astonished to see a magnificent tiger emerge in the moonlight! It was the purest white, with stripes of sapphire, and its eyes gleamed with a mysterious light.

Drawn by a strange power, the prince unlatched the window and climbed out. With the night winds ruffling his hair, he grasped the thick leafy vines clinging to the tower, and began his long descent.

When at last he reached the lower wall of the palace, the prince saw the white tiger waiting below, its eyes shining like gold. Without faltering, he leaped onto the tiger's back, and together they plunged into the jungle.

All through the singing night, the white tiger ran—beneath dark ledges and shadowy trees, through deep ravines, across rivers as black as onyx. As they raced on through the moonlight, the prince saw that the rivers had begun to run dry, and the trees were thinned and dying. With the first pale light of morning, their journey ended, and the tiger allowed the prince to dismount.

Prince Sanjay wandered over the parched and wasted land. In the distance, he could see many people crowded together on the bare, dry ground. As he drew nearer, the sounds of crying and wailing reached his ears, and a feeling of deep compassion flowed through him.

Never had the prince heard such sounds before, nor seen such poverty. The people were starving. Hollow-eyed and gaunt, they could only stare at him as he passed. Sanjay felt ashamed to walk among them in his fine garments. Gathering his silken stole, he gently laid it over three small children who huddled at his feet.

They had come upon a land afflicted by a great drought. Prince Sanjay looked around uneasily, and wondered why he had been brought to such a desolate place. He turned to speak, but the white tiger was gone. It had vanished with the night.

All day he walked the barren land, until the fiery sun at last sank behind the dusty hills and a golden moon came peering through the haze. In its light, the prince saw the white tiger waiting. As the moon broke free from the hills, the eyes of the tiger glinted gold. With one last anguished look toward the starving people, Sanjay mounted the tiger's back, and was spirited away.

Toward morning, the familiar mountain loomed ahead, and Prince Sanjay saw before him the gleaming towers of his father's golden palace. As the sky brightened, the tiger slowed its pace until finally, at the foot of the mountain, it stood still. The moment the prince dismounted, the white tiger vanished.

The prince had barely surmounted the wall of the palace when he was seized, and brought before the Emperor. To his surprise, his father seemed older than he had remembered.

"Ah, Sanjay, my only son!" sneered the Emperor. "At last you oblige me with your return . . . after these seven years!"

The prince was astounded to learn that he had been away for so long a time. In what had seemed to be but one night, his forty-nine sisters had all married, and left the palace for homes of their own. His seven mothers, too, had gone, for the Emperor had declined their company, choosing to spend all his days alone in the golden temple.

For seven years, the Emperor had knelt before Nurvah, begging for the return of his only heir, swearing, as before, to share his gold with the poor if his prayer would be answered.

Now the prince had returned, and the Emperor had one more chance to keep his word.

Prince Sanjay at once told his father what he had seen: "Beyond these walls of gold, beyond the jungle, there is untold devastation across the land. Father, you must help the starving people of the desert."

"It is not *my* stomach that is empty," replied the Emperor.

"But Father," begged the prince, "little children have nothing to eat! Can you not feed them? Will you not help?"

"Enough!" shouted the Emperor. "Such talk does not please my ears. Nor does it please me that my son has not yet learned obedience." Then, pointing a bejeweled finger to the ceiling, he commanded angrily, "Go now, to the tower! And remain there as I have decreed."

The Emperor ordered heavy chains with double locks hung upon the door to Prince Sanjay's room, and all the vines that grew along the golden tower were cut down. With the prince thus secured, the Emperor saw no need to keep his promise to the god of Creation.

He had forgotten that the great Nurvah was also the god of Destruction.

That night, the moon rose full, laying a silver mantle upon the mountain. Prince Sanjay, gazing from his open window, looked down into the gleaming eyes of the white tiger.

As in a dream, the moon appeared to grow larger and larger, and everything around glowed eerily in its light. The golden tower itself turned to sapphire and seemed to float away, leaving the prince abroad on the jeweled night air. Down, down through the moonlit mists he drifted, and found himself once more astride the back of the white tiger.

Suddenly, a deep rumbling was heard, like the sound of thunder. Yet the moon and stars were overhead in the clear, midnight sky. The rumbling grew louder. As the tiger carried him away, Prince Sanjay turned to look back . . . .

There, from the top of the mountain, billowed a great black cloud. As the prince watched, it darkened the sky and covered the moon. Then all at once, the cloud ignited to a fiery gold, and in its midst there appeared a fearful visage—the image of Nurvah! A terrible roar filled the air as the mountain erupted, spewing forth a fountain of liquid gold. The palace, and all within, was gone.

For seven days and seven nights, there poured forth a great river of molten gold. After a long while, the rich lava cooled, and all across the land lay a thick cover of pure gold.

Prince Sanjay called upon the poor to cut the gold into bars. There were enough gold bars to trade for food and clothing and shelter for all. There were enough for the people of the desert, too. Workers dug deep wells and brought rich soil so that trees and crops could be planted. In time, the land became green and prosperous once again.

The people, in their gratitude, welcomed Prince Sanjay as their sovereign. They built a castle of stone for him and his family, on the very same mountain where once stood the golden palace. From there, King Sanjay ruled with justice and charity all his days.

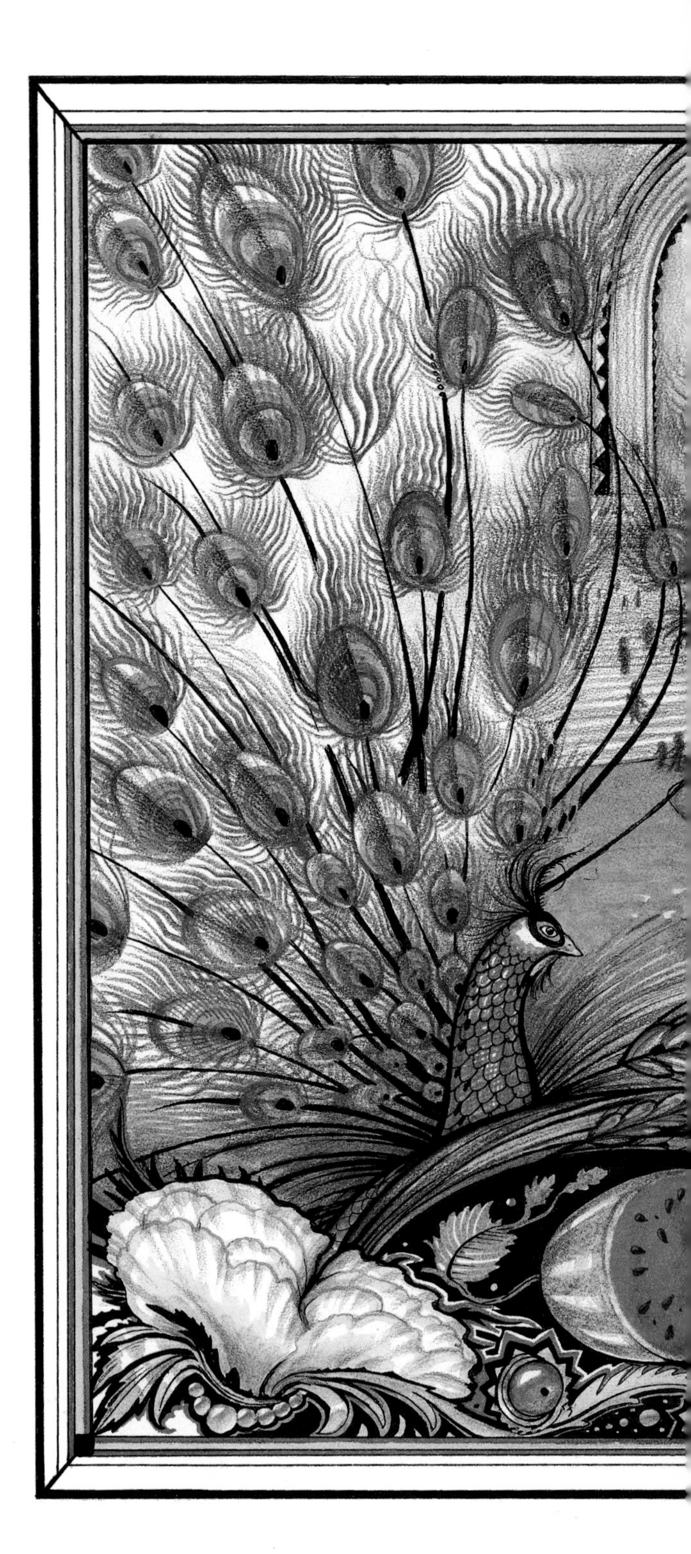

Still, when the moon comes full and spreads its silvery light upon the mountain, a chamber window opens. And somewhere, far in the jungle night, a white tiger runs.

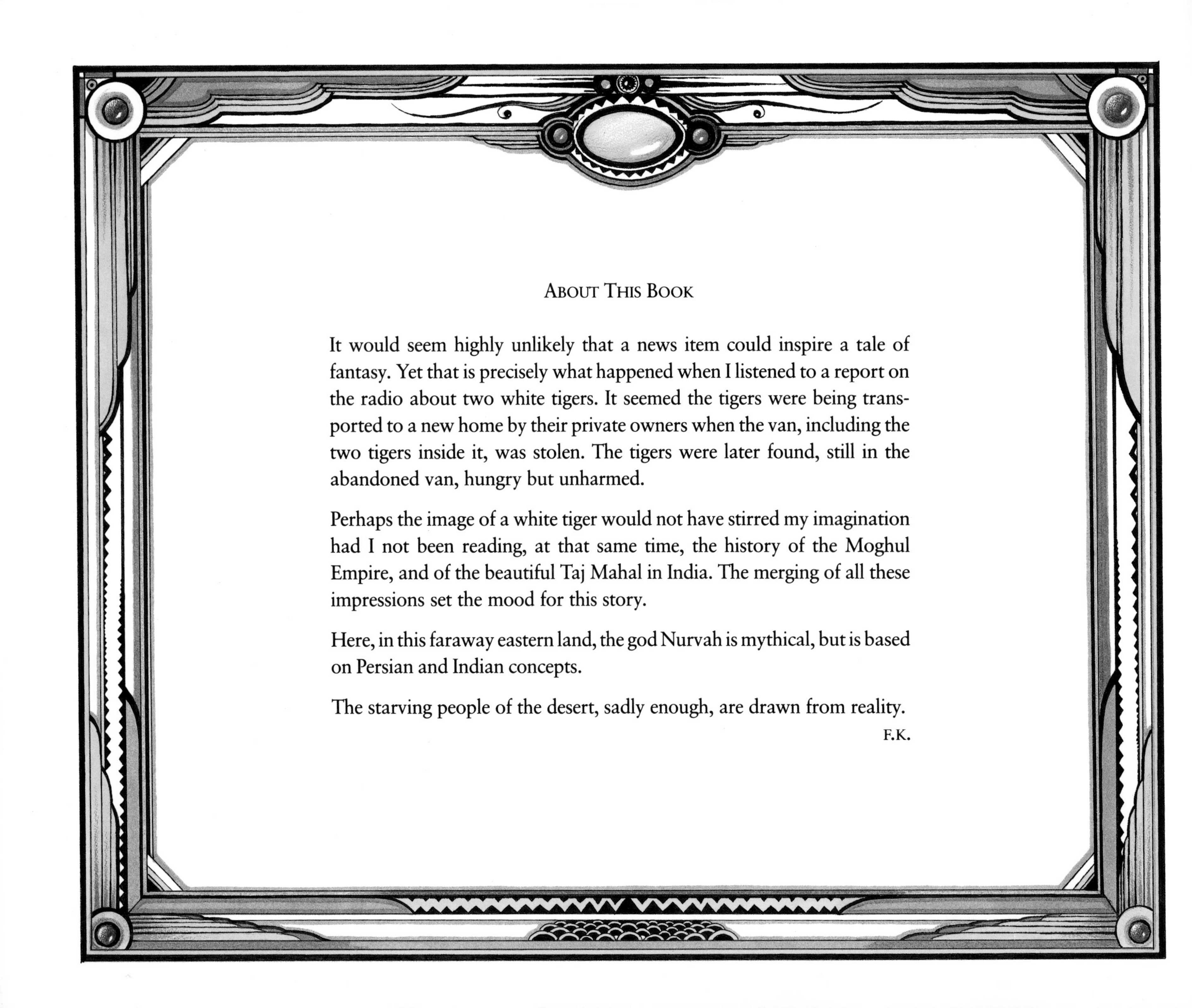

About This Book

It would seem highly unlikely that a news item could inspire a tale of fantasy. Yet that is precisely what happened when I listened to a report on the radio about two white tigers. It seemed the tigers were being transported to a new home by their private owners when the van, including the two tigers inside it, was stolen. The tigers were later found, still in the abandoned van, hungry but unharmed.

Perhaps the image of a white tiger would not have stirred my imagination had I not been reading, at that same time, the history of the Moghul Empire, and of the beautiful Taj Mahal in India. The merging of all these impressions set the mood for this story.

Here, in this faraway eastern land, the god Nurvah is mythical, but is based on Persian and Indian concepts.

The starving people of the desert, sadly enough, are drawn from reality.

F.K.